The Old Woman

M.J. Sherman

Printed in the United States of America

First Printing October 2017

ISBN 978-1-64136-441-6 Paperback

Published by: Book Services
                www.BookServices.us

Contents

The Old Woman

The night was clear and dark, the moon, a sliver hanging low in the night sky. The stars, although myriad, were glimmering weakly, unlike the sharp, unblurred points of light visible from my Colorado home.

I was walking along the road through the center of the small, quaint town in which I had spent my youth. There was only one lonely streetlight on the north side of the road, in front of the bank.

I stepped out of the dim circle of light cast upon the broken asphalt. I glanced down, looking for the safest way around the rough patches of pavement. Just as I came out of the faint ring of light, I glanced up, and there she stood: an old woman wearing a faded dress covered by a long, threadbare woolen coat with a scraggly fur collar and what once had been fur cuffs. Her shoes were shabby, the leather cracked, the soles broken and worn. Her hair was pulled back in a bun and covered with a tattered and faded black hat.

She stood leaning on a cane, one gnarled hand gripping it hard enough to turn her knuckles white. She had her back to me. There was something oddly familiar about her. I couldn't imagine why that should be, but nonetheless, I felt as if I knew her, even though I couldn't see her clearly.

As I stood there wondering, she turned and beckoned to me. I felt drawn to follow her, but something kept my feet stuck to the ground.

Our eyes met and held for a moment, then her hand dropped; she turned away from me again, and vanished.

I had come here for no other reason than to see if the town had changed over the years. My expectation was to stay only long enough to find out if it was as I remembered it, to see if our house was still there. Though I had no idea why, as I had no fond memories of it, or any reason to come back, it pulled me to itself.

The town looked and smelled much as it had when I lived here. The vintage buildings had not been replaced or renovated. The faint smell of molasses from the grain elevator still floated in the air. I had been gone for 15 years. Despite my lonely childhood, I had felt a need to come back, if only for a short time.

I went first to the city park. There was the band shell, where I had spent untold hours alone with my books and my imagination. Actually, it wasn't the band shell itself that evoked the nostalgia, but the area beneath the stage. The area could be accessed through an unhinged section of lattice on the south side of the structure. The rest of the base was vertical wood slats.

I stooped and crept into the space. I was a grown woman now, but the child in me was immediately back hiding from the big, bad world that I wanted to escape. This rough octagon still made me feel safe. It had been more of a home to me than the house that Lucille and I lived in.

After my father left, Lucille just gave up. She couldn't see any reason to even get up in the morning, much less take care of a small, bewildered child, especially one who reminded her, every day of the man who had walked out on her.

Lucille and I moved to New Holstein after we were forced to leave the house that my father had mortgaged. He had been unable to refinance it after his gambling finally caught up with him. Lucille packed up the few necessary items that we needed to survive and started driving. There was no reassurance that our lives would be any better when we arrived at wherever our destination might be.

I guess Lucille just drove until she got tired of going farther. "This is where we stop," she announced abruptly. "I've driven as far as I can."

I will never forget that trip. I was only five, though smart enough and tall enough to pass for seven. We stopped only for gas and food, or when I simply couldn't go one more mile without a bathroom break. We didn't stop at restaurants or diners. We stopped at gas stations and bought only what I could find while Lucille was in the bathroom.

I have no memory of the town we came from or the house we had lived in. I only remember the litter on the floor of the car, the way the vehicle was permeated with stale cigarette smoke.

Our move was a silent one. Lucille and I couldn't find anything to talk about that would make our lives better or the present more bearable.

I had already lost my father, and when my mother finally broke the silence, I knew I had lost her too.

She announced that I was not to call her Mom, or Mother, or Ma. She would be just Lucille from now on. She would provide what she could in the way of meals, and she'd see that I had a roof over my head, but I should not expect more that that. It was all she could or would do.

I dragged myself to school most days, but sometimes I just couldn't face the embarrassment and the snide comments of my classmates. I often had no clean clothes to wear and no lunch money or food to take with me.

As I grew older, I learned to put my head down and push through whatever problems arose. I was a good enough student that, even though I missed a fair amount of school, I got through it all at the head of my class. Valedictorian, but miserable.

When I turned 14, I procured a couple of part-time jobs that allowed me to buy clothes at the thrift shop. Mrs. Johnson, the owner, often gave me an extra discount on the already low-cost clothing. She said that she couldn't afford to hire me, but that if I would like to help her after school, I could have my choice of the clothing before it was put out on the racks.

I also dusted and scrubbed floors at the grocery store. Mr. Bertram usually sent me home with food that was nearing it's expiration date. He often had a heel of meat that was too small to sell or was on the verge of spoiling.

One day, after I had worked at the grocery store for almost 6 months, Mr. Bertram asked if I would like to take on more responsibility. "You're such a good worker that I would like to hire you. I can't pay you very much, but I sure could use the help."

"But you're already paying me. You're giving me food." His reply surprised and humbled me. "Your working here means I can go home and spend time with my family, and I'm happy to pay you for that."

I never earned a lot of money, but I made enough to keep some food in the refrigerator. Lucille bestirred herself enough to eat what I brought home, which meant I still didn't get enough to eat.

When I turned 17, I made a decision: I was leaving New Holstein. There was no reason for me to remain. I decided to buy a bus ticket to whatever city was at the limit of what I could afford.

When I got to the grocery store the next day, I told Mr. Bertram that I would be leaving soon. He said he would be sorry to lose me, but he understood.

On my last day, as I was putting on my coat to leave the store, he handed me an envelope. I thanked him, but I didn't open it immediately. I left the store and headed to the bandshell.

As I settled into my private place, I began to wonder if I had made the right decision. My hands shook as I opened the envelope.

Inside was a single sheet of paper—and fifty dollars! For just a moment I wanted to jump up and down and yell, letting the whole town know that I really was worthwhile and appreciated. The letter was short, but it made me happy.

Dear Mickey,

I hope this will help you on your journey. I'm sorry to lose you, but I'm pleased that you are going to look for a better life. You deserve it. Please remember, you're always welcome to come back to the store. There will always be a job here for you.

J. L. Bertram

In that moment, I knew that I would make it on my own.

The next morning I was at the thrift store when Mrs. Johnson arrived to open up.

I dug through the racks and found several dressy pairs of slacks and two pairs of jeans, a couple of good blouses, some t-shirts, and shoes. I plopped them all down on the counter and dug into my pocket for the money I had gathered up for traveling.

Mrs. Johnson folded all of the clothes, put the shoes in the bottom of the bag, the clothing on top, and came around from behind the counter with an empty bag under her arm. She took my hand and led me back to the racks where she started taking clothes off hangers. Once or twice she paused, looked closely at me, took an item from the rack, held it up in front of me and either shook her head and put it back, or indicated that I should put it in the bag with the other things.

When she was satisfied with the clothes, she took me to the shoe section and indicated several pairs that I should try on.

By the time she was finished, I had two paper grocery bags full of clothes and another bag that contained two more pairs of shoes and a week's worth of underwear. I stood there for a moment, embarrassed, and said, "But Mrs. Johnson, I don't have enough money for all of this." She looked at me and smiled. "You don't owe me anything, Mickey. These are my way of saying thank you for all of the work you did for me. And don't argue. You're going to need decent clothes if you're going to find a good job in the big city.

"Please, Mickey, let me do this for you"

I didn't know whether to cry or laugh, so I wiped at the tears pooling in the corners of my eyes, smiled and hugged Mrs. Johnson. As I turned toward the door with my bags, I saw a suitcase on a shelf near the entrance. It was twice the size of the one I had at home, and it looked almost new.

I walked back to the counter, dug $7.00 out of my pocket, and said, "This is for the suitcase over there," then turned and walked out the door.

The last two days had been amazing. I now had enough money to travel to wherever I decided and clothes enough to get me there. Despite my life with Lucille, I recognized that there were good people in this world.

As I walked toward the bus station with my new suitcase, I noticed a woman standing in the shadows. I hesitated a moment; she seemed familiar in some way. As I stood mulling this over, she disappeared. I didn't know if she had stepped deeper into the shadows, if she had walked away while I was pondering her familiarity, or if she had simply vanished. I shook my head to clear it, looked around, and, not seeing her anywhere, headed through the door into the station and my new life.

I approached the ticket window, and looked at the list of destinations, wondering which one I should choose. As I scanned the destination board, the name of one city appeared to glow: Bayfield, Colorado. It danced and shimmered in front of my eyes, as if trying to attract my attention. I had enough money for a ticket to Bayfield. As soon as I made the decision, the lettering ceased its glimmering. I guessed I had just chosen the city where I would be living for the next several years, at least.

As I seated myself in the departure section of the depot, I saw the old woman again. This time there appeared on her face a flicker of a smile and a nod of approval. She was beginning to freak me out. I never knew when I would look up and see the old woman standing near me. Who was she, and what did she want? I'd always escaped into my imagination from my unpleasant situation, but this seemed so very real. Maybe I needed counseling. Or maybe this was just some crazy old lady who lived on the outskirts of town as a hermit.

Just then the loudspeaker announced the arrival of the bus that would take me to my new home. The next three days were long and arduous. I spent most of the trip looking out the window. The scenery hurtling by had me mesmerized. At times it seemed to change in the blink of an eye, at other times there were only endless green fields and cows. But to me it was all fascinating.

After spending my life in a small town in the Midwest, never traveling more than 40 miles from home, to the big city of Fond du Lac, this trip across the country was exciting. It was also scary! I'd never even been to Milwaukee, let alone a neighboring state. Each time the bus stopped to pick up or drop off passengers, I got out and wandered around the town or city we were in. I always asked the bus driver how long we would be at this depot. He usually said, "I'll be pulling her out of here in 30 minutes on the dot!" I knew that if I was a few minutes late, he would find a reason to hold the bus for me.

The first driver was Harold. His voice was stern, but there was always a twinkle in his eyes and a slight upward curve to his lips when he spoke to me. I wasn't worried about traveling alone. I knew that Harold would look after me.

When we left Wisconsin wond headed west toward Colorado, I had no idea where exactly we were going. I had studied geography in school, of course, but seeing a place on a map and actually going there were completely different things.

We traveled through Iowa and Nebraska, then dropped southwest toward Bayfield.

Iowa was very much like Wisconsin, with trees and fields and cows. I asked whoever was driving this leg of the trip what was planted in the fields and the reply was, "Well, far as I know it'd be corn and maybe some wheat or alfalfa." Yup! Just like Wisconsin, except the cows at home were mostly dairy cows, and these were mostly beef cattle.

Nebraska was different. There were more open grasslands with broad vistas. I found it to be a bit scary—no trees and hills to make one feel protected from the outside world.

My travels ended when the last driver (I think this one's name was Eddy) shook me awake and said this was the end of the road for me; we were in Bayfield, Colorado.

I didn't know how long I had been asleep, but I woke to a whole new world. I was surrounded by nothing but huge mountains and trees. And the trees were mostly evergreens, not sugar maples.

I stumbled off the bus, a little giddy from the high elevation. Eddy hauled my suitcase out of the luggage compartment, waved, and drove away.

There I stood in front of a small old, grocery store, wondering what on earth I had done, coming to a place where I knew no one, with no idea what to do next.

I turned around and gazed at the building before me. I was just rooted in place, immobilized by uncertainty, when I felt a something nudge me, give me a little push toward the door. Looking back over my shoulder, I saw a shadow flicker, and again felt a push. I thought it must be the mountain wind. But a closer look revealed the old woman, *my* old woman, nodding and gesturing toward the door. I turned my head to look at the store, and when I glanced back, she was not there.

I hesitated a moment longer, and just as I had decided to head in a different direction, she pushed me through the door.

I stepped inside, set my suitcase down beside the door and began to wander down the first aisle. When I came back up the next one, the shopkeeper looked up, nodding his head, and asked if there was something he could help me find.

"Yes sir. My name is Mickey. I just got off the bus, and I'm looking for a place to stay. Just a room would be sufficient. If you know of a room that's available, I'd appreciate it."

He looked at me for just a moment, then smiled and said, "Young lady, I think I know just the place for you. Give me a minute, and I'll call Hester. I think she'd have a room for you."

I was wandering around, looking at what was available in the small, rickety old store, when the shopkeeper called to me. "Mickey, you're in luck. Hester has a room available and would be happy to show it to you. Turn left when you leave the store, take another left at the corner; it will be a big, gaudy house, the third on the right. Number 27. Could I offer you an ice cream cone or a soda?"

"Thank you, sir, a soda would taste very good right now." I pulled my wallet out of my purse, took out a dollar, and laid it on the counter. He pushed it back to me and shook his head.

"No, miss, this one's on the house." I started to argue that it wasn't necessary, that I could afford to buy it. He just got a soda out of the cooler, handed it to me, and replied. "She said you had been on a bus for 3 days and could use a cold drink."

"How did Hester know that I had been on a long bus ride?"

"Not Hester. The old woman who came in with you."

I nearly fainted on the spot. I felt my knees go wobbly and grabbed the edge of the counter in an effort to connect with reality. She had come into the store, showed herself to the shopkeeper, and she'd told him I was thirsty!

Who was this old woman, and why had she followed me here? This is eerie and unsettling.

I thanked the grocer, picked up my suitcase, and stepped out the door. I stood in the bright summer sun, under the bluest sky I had ever seen, shaking so badly that I thought I might fall. I shook my head to clear it, turned left, and found my way to Hester's house.

It was a huge two-story house, and—good grief!—it was painted lavender with pink shutters! But beggars can't be choosers, and it was the only place available, so I'd just have to pretend that the color didn't make me sick, and hope that Hester would rent me a room. And that I could afford the room.

Almost before I knocked, the door flew open. There stood what could only be described as the quintessential grandma, a plump woman with a flour-sack apron over her brightly colored, flowered, housedress. Her hands were covered with flour, and there was a substantial smudge of it on her nose as well.

The aroma wafting from her kitchen was absolutely heavenly! I thought it was apple pie, but I wouldn't swear to it. I had never smelled fresh-baked pie of any kind before. I smiled at Hester, trying not to drool.

"Hello, ma'am. My name is Mickey. The man at the grocery store called about my renting a room from you?"

"Yes, Mickey. William said he'd be sending you over here. I happen to have one room available. It's odd. The man who was in it suddenly decided that

14

he would be moving on. He had rented the room for six months, but he left after only two weeks without taking a refund. So the room is already paid for. If you're planning to stay for a while, the room won't cost you a penny."

Oh no, I'm sure that the old woman arranged this! This couldn't be coincidence. She made this happen.

"Come in, Mickey. I'll show you the room. I hope it's adequate. I haven't had the time to redecorate yet, but I'll get to it next week. In the meantime, the sheets are clean, and the room has been aired out. Would you like some apple pie? I just took it out of the oven. Run upstairs, first door on the right, and get settled in. When you come back down, the pie will be ready to eat.

Run along now. Oh, there are towels in the linen closet in the bathroom. You may use the blue ones."

I wasn't sure what to say. I had never experienced such kindness. I went upstairs to the first room on the right. It was huge! Bigger than the combined kitchen and living room in Lucille's house. I tossed the suitcase on the bed. (It was a double bed!) I dug out some clean clothes, then went searching for the bathroom.

Everything in it was outdated, the linoleum had more than a few worn spots, and there was a chip in the porcelain sink, but everything was spotlessly clean. I found the blue towels, big and soft, not like the thin, cheap, flimsy ones Lucille always bought.

I filled the tub with hot water and sank down into it. The bar of soap was brand new and smelled like lilacs. I hoped Hester wouldn't mind that I used her new soap.

I was so cozy and warm that I dozed off in the tub. I jerked awake. I had been in the tub for a half hour! I jumped out, pulled the plug, and dried off. I dressed quickly, wiped out the tub, hung my towel up to dry, and hurried downstairs, following the delightful smells to the kitchen.

Hester turned when I entered the room. She gave close scrutiny to what I was wearing: my new jeans, my light blue cotton shirt, and my new sandals. I guess I passed muster because she smiled and nodded towards the table. There were three metal chairs pushed in neatly around the oval table, which was covered with a bright yellow-and-white checked oilcloth. A vase full of pink roses sat in the middle of the oilcloth.

I pulled out a chair and sat down.

"Did you find everything all right? I hope the room is suitable. It was my daughter's when she lived here."

"Yes, ma'am. It's very comfortable. And bigger than any I've ever seen!" I blurted out. I hope it's all right that I took a bath. It felt so good and so relaxing. Oh— I used the new bar of soap I found in the soap dish. I will buy a new one if you want me to."

"No, I put it out especially for you. I hope you like lilac soap. It's my favorite. I always buy it, unless someone wants something different. And my name is Hester. You needn't be always sayin' ma'am like you were hired help or something.

If I'm being nosy, just tell me and I'll shut up. Do you have a job, or will you be needing one? My son, Matt, works in Durango. He could probably get you in at the Mexican restaurant where he works. I think I heard him say they were looking for a new hostess. The last one quit to get married; her baby was due, and they figured they'd better tie the knot before it came."

I just sat there at the table, listening to her rattle on, when I realized she had said something about a job and her son.

"I'm sorry ma'am— I mean, Hester, I guess I drifted off for a moment. I don't want to seem rude, but it's so nice to be off that bus. Did you say something about a job? I'm going to need one if I want to stay here. I don't have any kind of transportation, but I guess I could always hitchhike."

"Oh Lordy, child, you can't do that, it's too dangerous! I said my son, Matt, works at a restaurant in Durango and their hostess just quit. No loss there in my opinion! He could take you with him tomorrow when he goes to work, and you could see about the job. It pays well, and comes with uniforms. Or if that isn't to your liking, there are lots of stores always looking for dependable help.

As she finished talking, she plopped down a plate of fried chicken, mashed potatoes, and green beans, with a basket of still-warm, freshly-baked rolls, and tall icy glasses of tea. She placed another plate on the table just as the kitchen door opened to admit the most handsome man I had ever seen. He was about 5 foot 8 inches tall, had dark, almost black, curly hair, eyes the color of the sky on a clear day, and a boyish grin on his face. As Hester set down another glass of tea, he strode further into the kitchen, grabbed Hester around the waist and started dancing around the room with her. Both were laughing as they whirled around.

Matt caught sight of me, sitting in the chair with my mouth hanging open and a look of amazement on my face.

"Whassa matter, haven't you ever seen anyone dance around just for happiness' sake?"

It was said in jest, an expression of amusement on his face.

"No, I haven't," I said quietly. "It was just Lucille and me, and she never danced, or laughed."

"Oh, I'm so sorry. That was rude of me. You must be Mickey." He stuck out his hand. "Hi, I'm Matt. Have you tried that fried chicken yet? It's the best you've ever had, or I'll eat my hat."

I looked at his merry face, punctuated by the twinkle in his eyes, and burst out laughing. "Well, you'd better grab that hat and start eating. You may want to put gravy on it. I've never had fried chicken, so I wouldn't know if it was the best or not."

The smile faded from his lips, and the twinkle disappeared from his eyes. "I guess I'd better stop talking. I seem to be putting my size nines in my mouth today. I was just excited because I got a promotion at work today. I'm now the day-shift manager."

"Oh, then I guess I don't have to apply for the hostess job, since I have an "in" with the manager."

He looked at me for a short moment, then the twinkle reappeared, and the most beautiful laugh filled the kitchen. He sat down and started chowing down on the food his mother had set on the table when he walked in.

"Eat it while it's hot, best that way." I looked up from my plate. Matt's eyes were boring into me like drills. There was a strange, caring look on his face, then the whisper of a smile, before he took another bite of his chicken.

The three of us spent the evening talking. At about ten, Matt left and Hester and I went upstairs. Hester had given me an alarm clock, and I set it for 6:00 a.m. I didn't have to be ready until about 7:30, but I wanted to put all my things away, and I wanted to walk to the store before I left for what would be my first day of work, if I were hired.

William was just opening the store when I got there, and we walked through the door together. I picked up a small basket, and began to collect some things I needed. As I reached the counter, Matt arrived.

"Don't worry about food; you get that at the restaurant. All your food is free."

"That's all well and good, but I don't have the job yet. I'll have to have an interview with the manager first."

"Don't worry, Mickey," he chuckled. "I know the manager very well. He'll hire you."

"But he doesn't know if I can even do the job yet. And I don't know myself if I can do it, or if I even want it.

We looked at each other and broke into easy laughter.

I took my things back to the house, and Matt and I made the twenty-mile drive to Durango. He pointed out the local landmarks and told me about some interesting things to do, before we pulled up beside a brick building on Main Street. As we rounded the corner, I saw the sign for Pancho's Villa. When we stepped through the door, I found myself inside a bar, really more of an Old West saloon, called Pancho's. I turned to look at Matt, a question in my eyes.

"It's downstairs, there's another entrance to the restaurant. I just wanted you to see this. Lots of people come to the bar for drinks, then go downstairs to eat. Part of your job will be to get them down there when their table is ready."

"Does that mean I've got the job?"

"I'll recommend you for it. I think the manager will listen to me. Consider yourself hired. "

We clattered down the steps, laughing.

Pancho's Villa looked like it had been picked up lock, stock, and barrel from a Mexican village and tucked into the room under the bar. It was a bona fide Mexican cantina.

Matt and I worked together five days a week. That led to dating, and dating led to marriage. I'd lived in Bayfield five years when Matt and I bought Pancho's Villa. We were a great team, and people flocked to the restaurant. People liked me, actually *liked* the girl who had been an outcast in high school. But still, there was an unresolved ache in my heart, just under the surface.

Matt and I were successful, and we sold the restaurant five years later. It was at that point that I decided I would like come back to New Holstein. I don't know why I could possibly want to return to a place that, except for a very few people, held nothing but unhappiness and bad memories. Nonetheless, I felt a need to return. So Matt and I packed up the car, kissed Hester goodbye and drove off to Wisconsin, camping along the way.

This time, I was seeing the country from a car, not from a bus. We took all the time we wanted, doing lots of sightseeing and shopping in far too many tourist-traps, where we bought silly, cheesy things. We acted like young newlyweds.

Then when we got here, to this little town in Wisconsin, my mood changed dramatically. I felt excited, nervous, happy, sad and angry, each emotion fighting with the others to come to the forefront of my mind.

As we drove into New Holstein, I realized that I had tears running down my cheeks. I looked to see if there was anything left from my childhood. All of a sudden I saw it.

"Matt, stop the car. That's where I worked when I lived here. I have to see if Mr. Bertram is still there."

Matt got out, came around and opened my door, as he always did, and then, when we reached the store, he opened that door too. I nodded at him and smiled, our way of acknowledging little acts of kindness in the other.

I stopped in my tracks, and Matt bumped into me. There behind the counter stood the man who had given me the confidence I needed to make a life for myself.

"Excuse me, I'm inquiring about a job. Would you have one available?

He looked up from the papers he had been perusing. I saw his face go from questioning, to disbelief, to joy.

"Oh my gosh! Is that you, Mickey? I can't believe it. You came back. I was afraid you had gone out of our lives for good. I told you that there would always be a place for you here. You and your— husband?" He looked at the wedding band on my finger and smiled from ear to ear. "You are both welcome here any time."

"We'd like to have you come by for supper, if you would. There's so much I'd like to ask you."

I looked at Matt and he smiled at me. I knew that my acceptance of Mr. Bertram's invitation would be fine with him.

"Thank you, Mr. Bertram, that would be wonderful, but could we make it tomorrow night? I'd like to wander around town and see if the past is still here or if everything is gone. Besides, I'm sure your wife would like a heads-up before we descend upon her quiet, ordered household."

He stepped around the counter, shook hands with Matt and folded me into the biggest, friendliest, most wonderful hug I had received in a long time.

"Tomorrow evening will be fine. How about six o'clock. Of course, you want to see the town. I'll tell Mrs. B that you're here. She'll be thrilled to see you again.

We checked in at the motel. Somehow, sensing my need for healing, Matt said I should just go and do whatever I needed to do. He would be here when I got back.

It was coming up on dark when I left the motel. I hadn't been sure if I should be wandering around town by myself after dark, but I had to do this. After my visit to my secret hiding place under the band shell, my feet started moving of their own volition; they propelled me down the street, independent of my will. I realized that I was headed to my childhood house.

I didn't think of it as my *home.* It had never been a home to me. It was just the place I slept and where Lucille expected me to be.

The house was still there, and although it seemed impossible, it was in even worse condition than when we moved into it.

I didn't go up to the house. I didn't care to see it again. I remembered exactly what it was like to be there. I wasn't even curious to see if Lucille was still around.

I turned and headed down the street. I stopped beneath the lone streetlight to look around. The night was clear and dark. And there she was, the old woman! As I stood there, she turned and beckoned.

Why was she here? Who was this old woman? Who *was* she? Was she Lucille, trying to help me after all these years, or an ancestor—the ghost of a grandmother, perhaps—, or just my inner self, looking for guidance and clarity?

I waited for a moment, and when she turned, I ran to where she was standing.

"Who are you? What do you want?" I cried.

She didn't answer. This time, as she started to fade away, I reached out and touched her sleeve. I could feel the thin material of her dress, the fringe of her shawl fluttering against my hand. The streetlight brightened momentarily and then we were in inky blackness. I couldn't see her, but I could still feel her bony arm beneath my hand. The wind was blowing my hair around my face, as the woman's skirt wrapped itself around my legs. All I could do was stand there gripping her arm while everything swirled around me.

I wasn't in New Holstein anymore. I was in a rundown, abandoned house. The only things that were still intact were the fireplace and the huge iron pot used to cook and heat water.   And, of all things, a snow globe. I felt a strange shiver run down my spine. This place was grabbing me by the heart and I was, at the same time, repulsed and angry.

The snow globe shimmered. I reached out and picked it up. As I tilted it, I heard what sounded like shouting. There was a momentary swirl of mist and a man's voice, loud and angry. "… told you that I wanted my supper *on* the table when I came home! Are you stupid, or what?" Then the voice of a young girl, "I'm sorry, Daddy, I'll try to do better."

"Where's your mother? Why isn't she out here doing this work? She's as useless as you are!"

"She said she was sick, and she told me to get your supper ready. I tried, but there wasn't anything much to fix."

The girl ducked out of the house. At this time, whenever "this time" was, the house was in marginally better condition than when or where we were now.

The snow globe glimmered again, and I was transported to a scene perhaps ten years later. The same girl, now a young woman, was sneaking out of the house with a stunningly handsome young man. He wore a new, but obviously inexpensive suit, in which he looked decidedly uncomfortable. When he saw the girl, his face changed dramatically from fear to disgust to a leer that would make any woman run as far and as fast as she could. Nevertheless, whoever she was, this young woman looked adoringly at him.

They got into a run-down, rusty, formerly red, truck. Just as they disappeared around the bend in the road, the girl's father dashed out onto the porch, screaming, cursing, and shaking his fist. "That whore will never set foot in this house again. I spend my time working my life away for her, and she runs off with that hound dog. The ungrateful witch!"

By this time Mickey was weary and asked, "Are you showing me these visions, so that I will understand something important?" The old woman, still holding onto her arm, gave Mickey a slight smile and a shadow of a nod.

"Is this young woman Lucille?"

The old lady nodded her head a little more earnestly, and her smile broadened a bit.

"You're trying to show me why Lucille ended up a bitter and angry woman?"

Another nod, this time the movement was so vigorous that her thin, scraggly hair swirled in a cloud around her head.

She nodded again As I reached out to pick up the globe, the old woman touched my hand and nodded at the globe. She apparently didn't want me to pick it up. She wanted me to touch it. Not pick it up, just touch it.

My fingers tentatively touched the glass. The scene returned to the young couple in the truck.

"Where are we going, Joey? Are we eloping or what?"

The only reply from Joey was a sneer and a grunt. His only aim was to get Lucille off where he could have his way with her. Where her old man couldn't stop him. He didn't particularly like this girl. He just wanted an easy conquest with no interference from anyone.

They drove through the countryside, Lucille chattering on about nothing and Joey beginning to wonder if he should just kick her out of the truck and find easier pickings. She was hardly worth the trouble, but if he tried anything nearer to her home, her dad would literally kill him. So he would have to go somewhere else, pretend to marry her, and after a few days leave her, and go back home.

He didn't care at all what happened to her. It wasn't like they cared about each other. She was just the means of getting back at that horrible old man of hers.

Taking his daughter was the best revenge he could think of. The old bastard was a mean son of a gun, and he deserved to get back what he meted out. You didn't go around ruining a person's life just because you didn't like them.

Lucille's father had made public accusations about Joey—that he had stolen the old guy's watch and some money. The truth was that Bud had gambled it all away and needed a justification for why it was gone. He didn't have the guts to admit that he had lost it, so he blamed the only person he could find the courage to accuse. He was a classic bully and no one liked him, so he was obnoxious and belligerent because it made him feel like a big man.

Bud had just about run out of people he could push around when Joey had the bad fortune to look crosswise at Lucille. Bud didn't particularly care at all about Lucille. She was just someone he could bully into doing his bidding and not get a bunch of sass in return.

He had tried to use Joey in that way, but when Joey wouldn't knuckle under, Bud wanted revenge, and Joey became the scapegoat for his anger. He told the sheriff that Joey had stolen his stuff. The sheriff had questioned Joey and released him with a warning to stay out of trouble. It was all just a façade. The sheriff knew that, although he was a wild kid, Joey hadn't stolen Bud's things. He knew exactly where the money and the watch were. They were in the sheriff's pocket. He had won them from Bud the night before, but he had to at least act like he was doing his job.

So Joey had been made out to be a juvenile delinquent and put on probation. Well, he'd show Bud how it felt to be humiliated in front of everyone. He'd just take the only thing that Bud couldn't get along without: his "precious" daughter, his slave.

～

Mickey shuddered and dropped to the floor, exhausted. What a terrible life! That poor girl.

The old woman just nodded her head and again pointed at the snow globe. Mickey's voice quivered. "I don't think I can watch anymore of this."

The old woman began to shimmer and Micky closed her eyes and shook her head, a sob rumbled from her, and her knees gave out. She lay crumpled on the floor, trembling.

She felt a hand shaking her and looked up to see the old woman bending over her with a sad look on her face. She helped Mickey up, set her in a rickety chair, and handed her the glass globe.

Mickey shook her head and pushed the old woman's hand away, but she thrust it right back at her. She finally took the globe, sighed heavily, and opened her eyes.

~

Lucille was in a motel room. Joey's side of the bed was vacant. Lucille looked around the room in bewilderment.

She remembered leaving the house with Joey, her father standing on the porch shaking his fist, his face red as he screamed something at them. She remembered turning back and seeing a smile on Joey's face. It wasn't a pleasant smile, and for a fleeting moment she was scared. But she was out of that terrible house and away from her awful father. This situation couldn't be much worse. She had Joey, and they'd find a place to live and she could get a job.

Jerking herself into the present, she called, "Joey, sweetie, are you there? I'll be ready for breakfast in just a few minutes."

She got up, dressed, and knocked on the bathroom door. There was no answer. She knocked again and pushed open the door. The room was empty!

Maybe Joey went to the store to buy cigarettes; he smoked a lot. He'd lit his last one last night after they got here. He had wanted to go out and buy more, but she asked him not to. Couldn't he wait until morning? After all, this was their first night together, and she just wanted him to stay close. When she had asked him where they were going on their honeymoon, he just got a sly smile on his face and said, "That, my dear, is a surprise."

When they finally fell asleep, Lucille had a smile on her face, and Joey had a sneer on his.

She looked out the window. Joey's truck was gone! Maybe he had gone after cigarettes. He'd wanted to last night. Lucille sighed and sat down to wait for him.

After several hours she got very worried. She rose from the chair and went to the office. There was no one at the front desk, so she rang the bell.

Ralph came shuffling out from the adjoining room, glanced up and groaned, "You looking for that no-good husband of yours? He ducked out without paying for the room. I thought he took you with him, but I see he fooled you too."

"What do you mean, 'fooled' me, too"?

"He's gone, missy, skipped out on me, and never paid me nothin' for the room. You got the money for it?"

"I've got nothing. I left with the clothes on my back and a tiny case full of necessities. What do I do now? I'm stuck here, and even if I wasn't, I have no place to go. Joey was my escape from a bad situation. Now I'm in another bad one."

"Well, missy, if you really are in a predicament, I may be able to help you. I need some help here with the motel. You can pay for the room and maybe earn a little money to boot. Not a lot, mind you, but I would like an occasional night off, and you could handle things here while I'm out."

Lucille was stunned. She thought she was going to have to hitch a ride somewhere to try to find some work, and here was a job falling into her lap! "I'll do it!" she exclaimed.

She picked up on the work quickly and did it efficiently. Ralph was pleased. He could now spend more time doing what he wanted to do. He spent most evenings gambling. He didn't drink, he only wanted to gamble. It was the only thing he loved in life, and now that he had Lucille there, he had more time to do what he loved.

Eventually, he gambled away everything. He had put the motel up as collateral on his debt, and lost it almost immediately. When he got home, he told Lucille that he was going to have to leave. If she wanted to come along, she was welcome to.

"I have no idea where I'm going, but I ain't staying here in this dump of a town. I don't know if you're in any condition to travel, but if'n you are, you can come. You can do some of the driving. You do know how to drive, don't you?"

~

By this time Mickey was curled up on the floor, sobbing. The snow globe she clutched in her hand was blinking, the light getting brighter and dimmer with her weeping.

"Poor Lucille, she had such a hard life. I assume that by 'condition,' he meant she was pregnant. She was alone, working to survive, and pregnant…with me? No wonder she wasn't much of a mother, she didn't have the time to be. Lucky for her, Ralph was a decent, if uninterested, companion."

The globe flickered urgently in her hand. "No, I can't watch any more" The old woman nodded and pointed at the globe. "No, please. No more."

The old woman nodded, sharply this time. The globe vibrated almost urgently. Finally Mickey nodded. She tilted the globe and looked deeply into it again.

~

Ralph was not an unkind man, he was just indifferent about anything but his gambling.

Lucille decided it was better to go with him than to try to find a living here on her own. Besides, being pregnant and alone didn't strike her as a smart or comfortable idea. She loaded up the few possessions she owned, as well as the few things she had scrounged for the baby, and they set off.

Over the next four or five years they moved to several different cities and states. Always just a step ahead of the people looking for payment on Ralph's gambling debts.

Most of what he gambled with was money she earned at the few jobs she could find. Lucille managed to squirrel away enough to buy some food for herself and her daughter. The rest, Ralph took, saying it was for paying bills. He didn't tell her they were gambling bills.

Their life was not what you would call good. Lucille didn't have to suffer the abuse she had received from her father, but there was no joy or excitement in it. It was the kind of existence that dragged one down and left nothing in it to grab onto, no hope, no love, no enjoyment. There was just the everyday drudgery of trying to survive.

This was the life that Mickey was born into. She spent her first years mostly alone, Lucille seldom talked at all. When Ralph came home, he would ruffle her hair as he passed and mumble, "How ya' doin' kiddo?" He was never mean to her, but he never paid any more attention to her than that short greeting.

One day while she was playing outside, Mickey saw an old woman standing on the sidewalk in front of her house. When she stopped playing and stood up, the old woman lifted her arm and beckoned to her. Mickey wanted to run to the old woman, but she was scared to. As Mickey started walking toward the house, the woman disappeared.

Then one day Ralph left the house to "shoot the breeze with the boys" and never returned. Some policemen came one day and told Lucille that she'd have to leave, the house had been repossessed, and she needed to be out by tomorrow.

She packed up her things that night and, taking her daughter by the hand left that place for somewhere, nowhere… wherever.

~

Mickey sat up in the dim glow of the street light, looked around, shook herself and stood up. It took her a moment to remember where she was. She turned abruptly and ran back to her husband.

She had no idea how long she had been "gone," but she hoped she would find everything the way it had been when she left for her walk. As she neared the motel, she had a moment of trepidation, of unease. What if Matt wasn't there? What if she had been gone so long that he had given up and gone back to Colorado? What if this whole thing had been a dream, and she wasn't married to Matt at all, that she was still just trying to exist in this unhappy place?

She saw their car still parked in the same spot. Matt was still here. He was real. She entered the room, feeling nervous and afraid. He looked up from his magazine, smiled, and asked, "Is everything still where it was when you left it? Did you find your old home? I'd like to see it while we're here." Mickey stood frozen for a moment before throwing herself onto his lap and hugging him tightly.

She looked him in the eye and said, "Yes, yes, and maybe. Now let's go find something to eat."

Something snapped into place in Mickey that night. She'd been like an interlocking jigsaw puzzle with the key piece missing, the piece without which, it was impossible to make sense of the picture. The blank slate of her first five years was blank no more. Forgiveness and understanding filled her heart. As her husband wrapped her in his arms that night, she knew that she had utterly broken the long chain of unhappiness in her family.

She never saw the old woman again. She didn't need to.

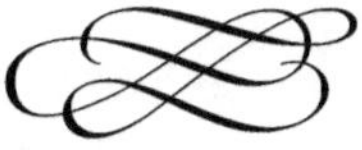

The Music Box

It was hard enough cleaning out their family home in preparation for the realtor's open house the next Sunday, but cleaning out their parents' bedroom was by far the hardest thing that Jacob and Jordan had ever had to do. They both had homes of their own, so they had decided it was best to sell this one. They agreed that they would do the hardest part first.

Everything in the bedroom was so very personal. Everything in the room had been touched by Mom and Dad's hands.

They paused outside the door, took two deep breaths, looked at each other for a fleeting moment, and then squared their shoulders. Jordan reached out with a trembling hand and turned the doorknob.

They were small boys again, sneaking into their parents' room, touching the things on the dresser, opening the closet door to stare in wonder at all of the amazing grown-up clothing hanging there. The floor was covered with shoes and boxes that they had never dared look into. They were well-versed in matters of privacy. The things sitting out could be looked at. The things put away or in closed boxes were private and so were not to be touched.

At exactly the same moment, they snapped out of their reverie and looked around the room. It looked exactly as it always had. Their mother's collection of perfume bottles was still mirrored in the glass top of the dresser. The last piece of jewelry she had worn lay beside her hairbrush, which still held strands of her beautiful auburn hair. Her glasses were still on the bedside table, along with the book she'd last been reading.

Jacob heard his brother's sharp intake of breath. Their father hadn't changed a single thing since their mother had passed away thirty years ago. Dad had lived in a shrine to Mom all these years!

Jacob glanced at his brother, shrugged, and pushed open the closet doors. "I guess this is as good a place to begin as any."

Jordan nodded and they began the difficult task before them, starting by pulling clothes off hangers and putting them in a bags to donate to the local women's shelter. Their mother would have liked that.

Jordan felt his brother freeze. He looked over to see Jacob standing there with something black draped over his hands. Jacob stood looking at the silky dress he held, a single tear running down his cheek.

"This was the dress our mom wore to our college graduation, when we got our doctorates. She was the most beautiful woman in the room that night…six months later she was gone. I was so proud that she was our mother. It's going to be a long, hard day, bro."

Jordan just nodded and continued pulling things off hangers.

The next thing he pulled off triggered a memory. This was the crazy shirt their father had worn on the day they tried to "get" their mother.

Olivia called the boys for breakfast. "We eat in ten minutes. Be late and you don't get any."

They rolled sleepily out of bed and, partners in crime, dashed to their closet and dug out some clothes. They each put on a pair of crazy, loud swimming trunks. One of them put on a striped shirt, the other a plaid one. They found two pairs of bizarre-looking socks their uncle had given them for their birthday one year. One pair had giraffes on them and the other had crocodiles. They traded one for the other, so each would be wearing mismatched socks. Then Jordan put on one of a pair of bright red high-tops and gave his brother its mate. Jacob gave one of his day-glo orange sneakers with Jordan.

When they stepped out of their bedroom, their father, Charles, was just coming out of the bedroom, dressed for work in his neatly-pressed khakis and button-down shirt, a tie in his hand. He stopped, gave the boys the once-over, smirked and went right back into the bedroom.

The boys clattered down the stairs and slid to a stop in the kitchen side by side. They didn't say a word.

Olivia turned down the heat under the bacon and glanced over her shoulder. There stood her sons, looking ridiculous and angelic at the same time. She opened her mouth to say something to them when Charles skidded in behind them, he too wearing a mish-mash of clothes. His socks didn't match, he was wearing sweatpants with his dress shoes and, worst of all, he was wearing a very loud Hawaiian shirt his brother-in-law had given him as a joke. Olivia shook her head and turned back to her breakfast preparations, her shoulders shaking with barely contained laughter.

"You have exactly five minutes to get into proper attire and be sitting at this table or you get no breakfast—and boys, if you miss the bus, you'll have to walk to school. I'm not driving you after this stunt. And that goes for you too, Charles!"

The three pranksters dashed back upstairs, put on their work and school clothes, and combed their hair. They were sitting at the table looking sweet and innocent when Olivia turned from the stove with a panful of bacon and eggs. She was trying so hard not to laugh, that she almost dropped the pan.

That was just one of the many memories that they relived that day, as they emptied the closet. It was also one of the saddest days they would experience in their lives.

They had gotten everything out of the closet and were ready to close the doors on that sad interlude when Jacob put his hand on Jordan's.

"Hey, bro, what's that, back there in the corner? It looks like some kind of box or something."

"You're right. How on earth did we miss that? It's big enough that we should have seen it. Grab it and haul it out."

Jacob picked up an exquisite wooden box. It had a design inlaid into the lid. The design was partially obscured by an envelope that had been stuck to it. The envelope had their names on it. They opened it to discover a letter from their father.

Dearest Jacob and Jordan,

I wanted you to have this box. It was the last gift I bought for your mother, although I didn't know at the time that it would actually be the last one. I expected to share it with her for many years.

I regret that we drifted apart after your mother died. I love you. I should have been there for you, but I was devastated, so I lied to myself. I told myself that you two had each other, so it would be easier for you to handle the grief.

I could think of nothing except leaving this house. So much of Olivia remained here that I felt I would suffocate if I stayed.

Jordan, climb down off your high-horse. I just meant that my grief was so strong that I had to decompress from her death. I found it almost impossible to do that when every time I turned around, I saw her. So I did the only thing I could think of to do.

I decided to visit all the places we had planned to see after the two of you had left home to start your own lives.

When Olivia died, I thought I might too. So I chose to travel. I would still have her with me, but I could escape the pain of seeing her everywhere I looked.

I took the music box with me. It kept her close in my heart, but without the ache of familiarity. It felt like we were together again, making memories for our old age.

I hope this music box will help you hold her close. Please forgive me for my seeming indifference. That is not at all what it was. I just didn't know how to help you, so I took my grief and left.

Please know that I loved you both and was so very proud of you. A father couldn't have asked for better sons.

> *Your loving father,*
> *Charles*

~

The boys were fifty-two when their father died. Jacob and Jordan hadn't seen much of him in the past ten years. He had spent nine of those ten years traveling across the country.

Charles took early retirement and bought an RV, stocking it with all new kitchen equipment, dishes, and bedding. He took nothing from his home that would remind him of Olivia—except the music box. He would drive his RV to a general area, or to a specific place, and stay as long as it took to see everything that he and Olivia had talked about when they were planning their future.

The longer he could stay away, the better. When he was near Cody, Wyoming, a fellow traveler had mentioned the Buffalo Bill Center of the West. It was a place where he could spend at least three days and still find things to see. He eventually visited every museum in the United States and Canada, however small. He only returned to the family home periodically to check on the infrastructure.

Jordan and Jacob seldom heard from their father directly. The grandchildren would receive an occasional postcard from some interesting place, and the boys and their families always got birthday cards, as well as a card and a small gift at Christmas. The gifts for the grandchildren weren't always the most appropriate, because Charles had never met them. And Charles only called them once a year.

The boys worried about their father, but there wasn't much they could do about it, so they went on about their lives, hoping that there would come a day when Charles would tire of traveling and return home.

Theirs had been a close family. The boys knew that their mother would always be there when they came home from school each day.

Charles arranged his schedule so that he could go to as many of the basketball games, soccer matches and swim meets as he could. During the summer months, he coached whichever sport was in progress at the time he was available.

He took them camping in the summer and skiing when it snowed. The boys turned into good skiers and were offered scholarships to several colleges.

Olivia, being the only female in the family, held a special place in the hearts of her guys. She was an attractive woman, tall and willowy. She had shoulder-length auburn hair that glinted with red highlights in the sunlight. Her eyes were large, with an odd characteristic. One eye was green and the other was hazel. The effect, when she looked directly at a person, was rather unnerving, but it added to her overall exotic look and regal aura, and the guys adored her.

When the boys were young, she had only to turn those beautiful, oddly-colored eyes on them and arch one eyebrow, and they would cease and desist from any mischief in which they were engaged. If they were fighting or running around and yelling while she was working, she would merely turn her radiant smile on them say quietly,"Thank you, darlings," and the boys would be very quiet and respectful for the next hour or so.

She never had to raise her voice or do more than raise her eyebrow to get the desired response from them.

They were so enamored of her that they responded without having to think about what she was asking of them. They were happy to make her happy.

~

Charles was a member of a large and boisterous upper middle class family. He had four brothers, but no sisters, and as a result, he was very shy around women. He was interested, but had neither the nerve nor the familiarity to interact with them. It wasn't until he went to college that he finally screwed up the courage to approach, much less talk to, a female.

Charles was tall, well built, and very handsome. He had thick, dark wavy hair, and eyes the color of storm clouds. His hair curled over his collar, and he had a neatly trimmed beard, of which he was very proud. He thought it made him look cool. He noticed Olivia almost immediately when she arrived on the campus. He noticed, but didn't have the confidence to approach her.

They crossed paths often in their college years, simply nodding or saying hello as they passed each other.

He was drawn to her, silently admiring her and the stylish cut of her clothes—no bluejeans and baggy shirts for a woman as fine as she. She strode across campus with a confidence he simply couldn't muster.

Olivia grew up as the only child of older parents who had to struggle to make ends meet. There was never anything extra in her life. She was loved, but her parents could only provide the necessities. She always had clean and neat, if not stylish, clothes. She was given ample, nourishing, but unimaginative, food. She vowed that when she was an adult, her life would be better than her childhood had been.

Olivia had been a a straight-A student and without the scholarship she received, she couldn't have attended college. She was not one to sit back and wait for things to happen. When she was a sophomore in high-school, she got a part-time job and saved every penny she could so she could buy clothes. She wanted to look like a sophisticated woman when she attended college.

She majored in advertising and, after marrying Charles, she started a party planning company that she could run from home. It was called "Party Time."

~

With his head spinning from the words of their father's letter, and awash with remorse at not having reached out to him, Jacob cautiously lifted the lid, almost fearing that, like Pandora's box, terrible and horrifying things might fly out. Jordan gasped when he saw another envelope. It held a letter to their mother from their father.

Jacob laid his hand gently on Jacob's shoulder as he removed several sheets of paper, smudged, wrinkled, and torn. The letter had been handled often, and from the looks of it, often dampened with tears.

My Dearest Olivia,

A box arrived today. It was to be your birthday gift.

It is 10 ½ inches deep by 11 ½ inches wide by 5 inches high. It is made of walnut and teak. The walnut is inset in a star patten on each of the four sides. The teak fills in the spaces around the points of the stars. The lid is made of teak, inlaid with a mother-of-pearl gardenia.

There is a small crank on one end of the box and a switch on the bottom. When the switch is flipped and the lid is lifted, it plays your favorite song, "Smoke Gets In Your Eyes."

The crank on the end scrolls pictures of our favorite family pictures. One of my very favorite ones is of you carrying Jacob and Jordan on our first day as a family.

Your smile said love and excitement, your eyes said scared! You were the best mom from day one. The boys got all the love they could ever want!

As I scroll through the photos I see more of my favorites:

You, with the boys at bathtime when they were just old enough to sit up on their own. You were soaked, looking like you had just stepped out of a lake. Jordan had foamy shampoo on his head; he looked like he had curly white hair.

Then there's a photo of you and the boys playing with the puppy, the one that the boys said "just followed them home" from the neighbor's house.

You, throwing a Frisbee for the now full-grown yellow Labrador, Spot. Remember what fun you had naming him Spot, when he didn't have a mark on him?

I look at the pictures of the boys at their college graduation and I remember ours.

I watched you walk across that stage with your confident stride and your head held high and I remember thinking, "I'd sure like to get to know that beautiful woman, but she is way out of my league."

Imagine my surprise when, six months later, you actually agreed to go on a date with me!

Now all I have left are these photos.

I was planning on sharing them with you for another thirty years. But you are gone now, and I have no one to share them with.

I can only relive them by myself, always wishing that you were here to enjoy them with me.

You were, you are, and you always will be the love of my life. I don't know how I'll go on without you, or if I even want to.

We often talked, after the boys were tucked into bed, of all the things we wanted to do after they left home. We were going to travel the country, seeing all the sights and visiting all the amazing places that were calling to us.

Now, there are no sights that I want to see, except you.

Six months ago, you were so vibrant and alive. Then that tumor reared its ugly head and devoured my only love.

It was so sudden. I was so shattered that I had for-gotten all about the music box. When it arrived, on your birthday, I considered just throwing it away. It was so hard to look at, that I didn't know if I could keep it around. It would always remind me of what I had lost.

I saw it at one of the conventions I seemed to be spending my life attending. That particular one was in downtown San Francisco. It was a foggy and rainy day. I was missing you, so instead of having lunch, I went for a walk.

I wasn't even thinking about your birthday yet. But when I passed the little shop that sold music boxes and snow globes, this box caught my eye. I took one look at it and knew it was the perfect birthday gift for you. It was made in Italy, and they wouldn't part with the display sample. However, they had more coming in and promised to have this delivered on your birthday.

I spent hours going through those photos, the ones you had lovingly arranged and labeled. I had copies made of the ones I thought would mean the most to you.

Yes, that's what I was doing in my office all those long winter evenings. And yes, I wish now that I had spent those precious hours with you instead.

The boys took the things they wanted after the funeral and went back to their lives. I was left with the things they didn't want. Now I'm left with the memories encased in this music box.

I will mourn you for as long as it takes for the pain to stop. Then I will take this with me, and together we will do all of the things we had planned to do in our future.

Today is your birthday. The box arrived, too late for you, but in time for me to realize that we can keep our love alive.

> *Always and forever,*
> *Charles*

Jordan was the first to break the silence. "He really loved her! I've never read anything so beautiful! I thought he hated all of us."

"Jordan, do you realize that we are the same age that Dad was when Mom died?" said Jacob, choking back tears. "I saw them as just an old married couple. You and I were so young… I had no idea of the strength of the bond they shared."

As the two brothers held each other and wept, each realized that what they had expected to be an ending was only the beginning of a new and healing path, one that they and their families would walk together.

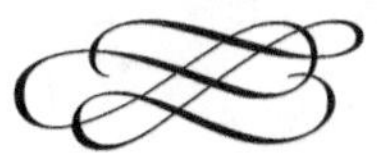

Monday's Flowers

Flowers are delivered to my house every Monday at one in the afternoon. Why? I have no idea, but there they are in a bucket beside the front door.

They are seasonal, the first ones of the summer might be red roses interspersed with delicate sprigs of white baby's breath. Then a bouquet of yellow daisies and sky blue larkspur might appear.

In spring, I find tulips, jonquils, sweet peas and my favorite, lilacs. Autumn brings amaryllis, mums and sunflowers.

I don't know who is sending them, or why.

The first Monday after I moved into the cottage, I was almost home from town when I spotted an old white van pulling out of my driveway. It turned left, away from town, and disappeared around a curve in the road.

~

I was on my own for the first time in forty years. Feeling that I needed a total change in my life, I decided to sell the condo that my husband—make that ex-husband—and I had lived in for all those years, and look for something smaller and more remote, away from the city and all the questioning and puzzled friends who didn't understand how John and I could split up.

I planned to buy a house in the small town of Whitby, a small town in Wisconsin, not far from the big city I had lived in.

I saw the cottage as I was driving into town. There was a sign beside the narrow, overgrown path to the house. *For Sale.* I turned in and stopped dead. There in front of me was, my house! I was sure of it.

It was a small bungalow, probably built in the 1930s. It had a roof of cedar shakes, leaded glass windows, and ivy growing up the pillars on either side of the steps. Although everything looked overgrown, the window boxes were filled with perky red geraniums, most likely the work of the realtor, and lavender, white, and pink phlox had gone wild along the base of the front porch and down the driveway. It was a storybook cottage and it called to me.

I backed out of the driveway and headed for town to find the real estate agent. I located the real estate agency on Main Street, parked, and hurried across the street, only to find a sign in the window: *Closed*

I turned, feeling sad and defeated. After the unpleasantness of the divorce, it didn't seem to take much to evoke negative feelings. I started across the street to my car when a woman passed me, said good afternoon, and unlocked the door from which I had just turned away.

"Oh, good, you're open!" She smiled, stepped aside, and waved me in ahead of her.

We shook hands and I introduced myself. "I'm Jennifer Logan. I've come to buy a house. We don't have to go looking, because I've already found the one that I want."

She nodded and asked, "Which house have you seen? Did you see the inside? And may I ask who showed it to you?"

"It's the small cottage out on Q Street. I saw the for-sale sign as I was driving into town and turned into the driveway. The place called to me. I knew for sure that it was the place I had been looking for."

She gazed at me briefly with a quizzical expression on her face, pulled a folder out of her file drawer, and paged through it.

She shook her head, stood up, and excusing herself, walked into an adjoining office. There was a rustling of papers, and then, in a moment, she returned with another folder, laid it on her desk and opened it to the page with the cottage on it. "Is this your house?"

"Yes! That's it. That's my bungalow!"

After we had talked for a few minutes, she suggested that we drive out to take a look at it. Finally! I was going to see my house! I could hardly contain myself during the five minute drive.

When we turned into the driveway, I immediately noticed the flowers on the front porch. They had magically appeared in the hour since I had first seen the house.

"Do you know anything about the flowers on the porch? They weren't there when I stopped by earlier. Maybe they were misdelivered."

Alice, the realtor, shook her head and said, "No, I don't know anyting about the flowers or why they might be here."

She led me on a tour of the grounds, the little woods full of early spring wildflowers: patches of white trillium, bloodroot, spring beauties, and wild hepatica. We peeked into the garden shed, with its potting bench, rows of clay pots, and garden tools hanging from hooks, all meticulously maintained. The path to the house was lined with beds of blue periwinkle.

The inside of the cottage was as quaint and charming as the outside. We stepped into a small, cozy living room. To the left was a narrow hallway that led to two small bedrooms and a bathroom. On the right was the kitchen with a cute little breakfast nook. Although the kitchen had been partially remodeled, the original potbellied stove remained. It couldn't have been more different from the sterile urban condo I had lived in for so long.

Directly across from the front door was a fireplace, also original, flanked by hand-hewn shelves. The house was warm and welcoming. And it would soon be mine! It was move-in ready. I could leave everything new and modern behind and start over without too much disruption. This place spoke to my heart.

Alice interrupted my reverie. "What do you think? Would you like to finalize this deal?"

"The sooner we can get everything settled, the better. Tomorrow?"

She laughed,"Well, I'm not a magician, but I'll get the paperwork started, and we'll see what can be done."

It was hard to drive away from the cottage. I wanted to be living here, not in transition.

I noodled at all of the things that needed doing: putting the condo on the market, moving the things

I wanted to keep into temporary storage, having my mail redirected to this small town…

I waited anxiously for three days. Alice called at last. The cottage was mine!

I moved in immediately. There were several things that I removed from the cottage right away: a large-screen television and a fancy new refrigerator among them. I ripped up the carpeting in the bedrooms to uncover beautiful hardwood floors. I replaced as many modern things as possible with things appropriate to the period in which the house was built, trying to be as historically accurate as possible.

Once I was settled in the cottage, I started going through all of the things I had hastily boxed up and put into the trunk of my car.

I drastically reduced my wardrobe. I wasn't going to need the dressy clothes that I had gotten for the political functions I was expected to attend with my husband. I didn't even miss them—the clothes or the functions.

I donated all of my fancy knick-knacks to a resale store and sold all my extravagant jewelry, except the heirlooms from my family.

I wasn't exactly sure what I wanted to do with my new life, but I knew that from now on, it would be my life and my decisions. There would be no more scheduled functions or luncheons.

The first Monday after I officially moved into my house was the first of October, so my first flowers were rusty orange mums with sprays of red, orange, and gold autumn leaves. I saw them sitting on the porch when I pulled into the driveway. I almost cried when I saw them. No one had ever given me flowers before. (That's right, my very important husband had never cared enough to buy me flowers.)

I carried them into the house and put them into a vase. I set it in the exact center of the small kitchen table. I knew that they hadn't been delivered for me. But just their being there made me feel special.

Early the next morning, I drove back to the city to sign papers on the sale of the condo and to tie up other loose ends, returning home about one o'clock. I turned off the main road just in time to see a white van turning out of my driveway onto West Q Street, the road that ran in front of my house.

I considered following it, but I had food to put away and some writing to do for the newspapers and magazines that I freelanced for.

As I made the turn off the road into my driveway, I saw the new flowers sitting in the bucket under the mail box. The old ones were nowhere in sight. The person who delivers the flowers, must also dispose of the old ones.

This Monday, the flowers were tall spikes of purple and yellow gladioli, with oak leaves and baby's breath.

The flowers always made me smile. I really wished I knew who was sending them. I wanted to thank them for the pleasure the flowers brought to my life.

I was out riding my bike one afternoon when the white van passed me going in the opposite direction. I continued pedaling down the road at a leisurely pace. He was driving relatively slowly, heading away from my driveway, so I casually followed him, feeling a little like a stalker or maybe a spy.

If he had looked in his rearview mirror, he would have seen an elderly woman bicycling innocently along. Nothing suspicious there!

About a mile down the road, the van pulled into an unpaved driveway, much like my own. It ended in front of an old, slightly weathered gray house.

There was nothing to indicate that it was anything more than an old, and not very well maintained, house. There was no flower garden, no greenhouse, no toolshed filled with a wealth of gardening tools. This couldn't be where the flowers came from.

I pedaled on by, so as not to appear to have been following him. But I needed to find out why he delivered flowers to my house every Monday. It was beginning to become an obsession with me. My experience with my ex-husband made me terrified of doing the most logical thing: going up and knocking on the door.

I turned around, pedaled back to my bungalow, showered, and drove into town. My first stop was at the post office.

I figured that they would be most apt to have information about the people they served and would know who the mystery deliveryman was.

I entered the post office and waited until it was my turn at the counter. I introduced myself ad explained that I was looking to get some information about the man who delivered flowers to my house every Monday. The gentleman behind the counter replied,"The man's name is Eugene Taft. He lives in the farmhouse that he was born in. I've been told that his parents are gone and he never married. He has no other family that I know of." That was the only information he had. He explained that he had only been at this location for five years and had limited knowledge of the people at the fringes of his territory.

I thanked him for his help and exited the building. I decided that the next place to go would be the grocery store. I felt rather guilty about just going in and asking for information, so I wandered up and down a couple of aisles and picked up a couple of items before I approached the checkout counter. After the usual pleasantries, I posed my question about Eugene.

The clerk's reply was about the same as the postal clerk's.

"He lives alone in the house he grew up in, the last member of his family, no brothers or sisters that I know of, never married. Heck of a nice guy. He'd do anything for anyone who asked for his help. Don't see much of him. He only comes in twice a month for groceries, always the same items, so I have them bagged and ready for him. He always pays cash, but never stops for conversation. Keeps to himself mostly. Drives around in that old white van."

"Do you you know anything about the van? There are no identifying marks on it except for the faded flowers on the side. Was Mr. Taft in the nursery business?"

The grocer just shook his head and chuckled. "Oh now, that was just something that showed up at Draper's Garage one day. Bob was going to scrap it. He asked Gene if he would haul it off to the scrapyard. Offered him twenty bucks to take it away. Bob could have done it hisself, but he figured Gene could use some extra bucks. The next thing we knew, Gene was driving it around. Guess he figured he could make some dough hauling stuff for people. Pay him a few bucks, and he'll haul it away."

I asked if he had any connection with any florists in the area. His said, "I don't know, but if one of them asked him to deliver flowers for them, he would."

I thanked him for the information and drove home, mulling over the information I had received.

I made it a point to be home the following Monday. I was outside pulling weeds when Eugene arrived with the flowers.

He pulled into the driveway, stepped out of the van, reached behind the seat, and picked up the flowers. He turned and started across the yard. He reached the porch, saw me working with the plants in front of the house, and stopped.

I looked up at him and nodded, "Afternoon, Gene." I went back to my gardening.

He stood on the bottom step, seeming to be pondering whether or not he should say something. He finally did. "Afternoon to you, ma'am." Then he continued up the steps, bent down, removed the old wilted flowers and arranged the new ones in the bucket. He stood, turned, and started toward the steps. Down he came, one-two-three. He came to an abrupt halt. I was standing on the flagstone just off the bottom step. If he stepped to the last one, he'd bump into me.

"Gene, my name is Jennifer. I'm the new owner of this bungalow, and I'm curious as to why you keep delivering flowers here. Don't get me wrong. I love them, but I am stumped as to why they are coming every Monday."

He stared at me for a long uncomfortable moment before he answered. "Well, ma'am, the gentleman who used to live here arranged with me to deliver them every Monday, no matter what.

"You see, him and his wife, they married late in life, and they bought this here cottage to live in for the years they had left. He loved her, and she loved him. And she just loved flowers, so he arranged to have fresh ones brought here every Monday 'cause that's the day they were married on. He wanted her to know that it would always be a special day.

"They were married for just about five years, you see, and then he passed on. His wife was truly devastated, but every Monday, when those flowers arrived, she knew that he still loved her, just as much as ever."

"But they're both gone now, so why are you still delivering them?"

"Because he was my friend, and he wanted them delivered as long as the money lasted."

Gene shook his head and went on, "Mr. McCallum didn't realize that his wife would die so soon after he did, but I had promised to keep delivering flowers as long as the money lasted, and that's what I aim to do. Now I have some furniture to pick up for a lady." He stood on the steps for a moment. I stepped aside and he proceeded to his truck.

I called after him, "You're a good man, Gene, a good honest man."

I've lived in the bungalow for two years now, and the flowers still arrive like clockwork at one o'clock every Monday afternoon.

One day, I had just gotten back from a trip to town. I climbed the five steps to the porch, my hands full of bags and boxes. I set everything down to dig out my keys and came face to face with three huge sunflowers framed by autumn leaves and tall spiky grasses.

I smiled as my heart filled with a profound happiness. I could honestly say that I never suffered from "blue Mondays" anymore. If Monday morning started out badly, it always improved with the early afternoon delivery of flowers.

One day I was working at the beautifully-carved wooden desk (I sold the glass and metal monstrosity that had been in the condo), and I reached into the top drawer for a pencil. I couldn't feel one in the front tray, so I reached toward the back of the drawer where I kept a supply of sharpened ones. Instead of a pencil, my hand touched what felt like an envelope.

That's odd, I didn't see anything in there when I stowed my supplies in the drawer...

I pulled out a faded and worn business-sized manilla envelope with what seemed to be a name written on it. The blue ink was badly faded. I couldn't tell if the name was Mary, Maria, or maybe Marie, but it hadn't been opened, so I figured that the woman never received it.

I thought I had heard Eugene refer to the woman who had lived here before me as Rachael. Either I was mistaken, or someone had left the envelope in this drawer before the McCallums had purchased the house.

Well, I guess it's time. I'm going to look into it.

I carefully slit the envelope open and even more carefully pulled out a sheet of yellowed and brittle paper. Slowly, so as not to tear it, I unfolded the sheet.

As I began to read, I realized that this had nothing to do with the McCallums.

It had been written by an earlier occupant of the cottage, a George Kraft, to his wife, Marie. (The faded name on the front of the envelope was Marie.)

Dear Marie,

You are meant to get this after I am gone.

I want you to know about a financial arrangement that I made shortly after we were married. I remember telling you about a sum of money that I was putting into a special fund. I put it into a trust fund for a nephew that I hadn't known about before.

I grew up as the only child, as I was led to believe, of moderately wealthy parents. When I was born, they set up a trust fund that I was to receive when I turned 25. The year I turned 24, I found out that I had an older brother named Ralph.

My parents had decided to wait to have children for several years—until they were financially stable. When my mother became pregnant within the first year, they decided to put the baby up for adoption. My father was just starting up a business, and my mother was barely 19. They just felt that it would be better to wait until they were more settled and secure to have children.

Ralph had been adopted four years before I was born. He had never been mentioned by my parents, for reasons unknown to me. The people who adopted him were farmers and had specifically asked for a boy. The farmer wanted a boy so he would have someone to help on the farm. His wife just wanted to adopt the child she couldn't bear herself. So Ralph spent his early life working for a father who had no real love for him.

When he turned seventeen, he had finally had it. He kissed his mother goodbye and moved away.

When Ralph met and married his wife Laura, he changed his last name to Taft. They had one son, Eugene. They lived a good life. Ralph bought a farm— farming was the only thing he knew how to do. Sadly, when Eugene was five, Ralph was killed when his tractor rolled over on him.

That was just after I had discovered that Ralph was my brother. I had found a letter in some of the things I cleaned out of the house after my mother died. She had written a letter to me, like I am writing this one to you, to be read after she was gone.

Well, back to my tale. When I found out that Laura had been left without any kind of support, I decided to give my trust money, anonymously, to the two of them. They were the only family I've ever had, except for you, my dear.

I hope that you won't fault me for making the choice that I did. I knew that the money would not be missed by us. We had more than enough of our own.

I set up the fund so that Eugene would be told about it when he reached the age of 25. I hope that I will live to see that happen, but if I don't, I would like you to tell him. I have sent a copy of this letter to our lawyer, so if you can't, he will.

> *Your loving husband,*
> *George*

I later found out that Eugene was told about the fund on his 25th birthday. The lawyer asked him what he wanted to do with the money. Would he like to invest it or maybe put it in an interest-bearing account? He'd said, "No, just leave it, there's more than I will ever need. I will just draw out what I need to live on. When I'm gone, it can go to help someone who really needs it.

And so, Gene went on living the life that he pre-ferred. He promised himself that he would find a way to thank the uncle he never knew. He decided to deliver flowers to the bungalow for as long as he could.

He had been reared to always be honest and to always do what you said you would.

So the flowers still arrive at the bungalow every Monday.

The December flowers so far have been, pine boughs with holly and red berries, then dusty miller with red bows and silver and red balls. I can hardly wait to see what will arrive on the Monday before Christmas.

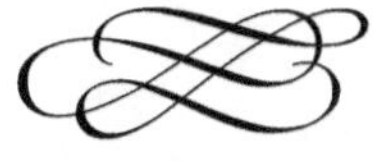

The Old Woman

Julie & Jacques

Julia Howard was 35 years old. She lived in a small apartment in a big city, she had a job she loved, her family was close by, but not so close that she felt stifled. She had her independence, but also the security and support of family.

She was tall and slender. She wore her hair, which was the color of a new penny, cut short. Her skin was clear and retained the look of a summer tan year-round.

Julia had a few close friends, and she had dated two men off and on over the last few years. But neither of the men was special enough to warrant a deeper, long-term relationship. Her heart just didn't respond to either one of them, nice as they were. So she was surprised at her reaction when she saw the return address on the letter that came in the mail. It set her heart to fluttering and her hands sweating. This had the potential of turning her life upside down. It could change everything.

She'd thought that she recognized the handwriting, and she had. When she looked closely at the smeared return address, she shivered—Jacques!

There wasn't time to read the letter now. She would be late for work if she did, so she tucked it into the inside pocket of her tote bag and set off for her office.

It was difficult to concentrate on the drawings on her desk. Her mind kept returning to the letter tucked into her bag. She hadn't thought about Jacques for years. Getting over him had been the most difficult thing in her life.

When Julia turned 21, her grandmother's birthday gift was a year in France in the small house in which Nanna had lived when she was young.

Nanna had fallen in love with an American businessman and married him. She had returned to America with him. They had made many trips back to France over the years, because Papa knew how much she loved her native country, and he wanted her to be happy.

When the house that Nanna grew up in became available, Papa bought it for her. After Papa retired, they spent six months of the year in her childhood home and the rest of the year traveling around France and the United States.

When Julia turned 16, Nanna and Papa began taking her with them on their travels. She usually spent a month or two in France with her grandparents and several more traveling around Europe.

The day dragged, and she simply couldn't concentrate on her work. The architectural drawings were just a series of abstract, unrelated lines to her. The building on her blueprint blurred in and out of focus as her mind jumped from work to the letter and back.

What could Jacques possibly have to say to her after all this time?

It had taken almost fifteen years to get over him. Why was he upsetting her life after all this time?

They had met during the year she spent in France when she was 21.

Jacques lived across the street from Nanna's house, and he knew her well. He wanted Julia to feel comfortable and welcomed, so he crossed the road and offered his services as tour guide, and finally, as her lover.

When the time came for her to leave, he tried to convince her to stay. They argued about her need to go.

In the end, he gave her an ultimatum: if she left, it would be the end of the relationship. She explained again and again, that she had just been offered a wonderful job, and if she didn't go back, it would be given to someone else. It was something she had worked so hard for during the last three years, and she didn't want to lose this opportunity. They could keep in touch. When she would come to Paris for her job, they could see each other, and he could fly to New York to visit her any time.

His reply had been, "Never mind. If you leave, it's over, forever." She cried and pleaded, but he wouldn't relent.

Julia returned home to start her new job. She sent Jacques chatty, friendly letters, but he never answered them. He didn't return any of her phone calls either.

At last she accepted that it was really over and got on with her life. Now here was a letter from him, after all these years.

When she finally got to take a break, Julia poured herself a cup of tea, locked her office door, and sat down in the overstuffed chair in the corner. She reached into the tote bag and pulled out the envelope she had tucked into the pocket earlier that morning. Her hand shook, and her heart beat rapidly as she held it. She carefully opened the envelope and gently unfolded the letter. A tear ran down her cheek when she saw his handwriting.

Scenes from their year together flashed through her mind.

A late supper at the small café just around the corner; strolls along the Champs Elysees and through the Arc de Triumph, holding hands and seeing only each other. They wandered through Notre Dame and gawked, like all the other tourists, at the Moulin Rouge.

Sleeping in on the weekends, listening to the city waking up.

Jacques had never stopped loving Julia. He regretted the stubbornness that had led to their separation, the pride that had led him to refuse to respond to her letters and phone calls. His heart ached with disappointment in himself, so when he got the news that he had only two years left, he immediately wrote to Julia.

My dearest Julia,

Please forgive me for being the stubborn dope that allowed you to leave my heart.

I wanted you to choose me instead of the job I knew you loved. When you didn't, I was devastated, and I took that anger out on you. I forced you to turn away from me instead of turning to me.

I thought you would come back to me after you had a chance to think it over. I expected to get over your leaving, but I kept stoking the fire of resentment. Every time I sat down to answer one of your letters or phone calls, intending to ask you to forgive me, the demon in my head beat down the love in my heart. I finally over-

came that demon, but by that time it was too late, you had stopped writing and you no longer called.

I suppose I should have tried harder to contact you, but I was certain that it was too late, that you had gotten on with your life...without me.

I did write to your grandmother for a while. Nanna kept me up to date on your life and activities. Eventually she too stopped writing, and I thought that you had asked her not to write to me anymore. Then I found out that she had passed away. By the time I knew that, it was too late. I wanted to fly to you to shield you from the hurt and sorrow. I knew how close the two of you had been, and I knew that her death must have been agonizing for you.

I had actually purchased an airline ticket to come to you when that demon appeared in my head again. It took me several months to subdue him and by then it was too late to be of any help. So once again, I let my pride and selfishness get the best of me.

Two years ago I fell ill, and I was diagnosed with a rare and incurable form of cancer. The doctor told me that I had four years to live, at most.

At my last visit, the doctor said I had less two years left, most likely, just over one.

I am writing to ask a favor of you. I would love it if you would consider coming here and spending this last year of my life with me.

I well send you an airline ticket (open-ended) I cannot die without showing you how sorry I am about the way I acted when you left. My actions caused you pain and I never wanted that. I'd like to make it up to you.

If you can forgive me, please call, and I will make all the arrangements for you. I would come to you, but I'm not allowed to fly anymore.

I am hoping to hear from you soon. Please, call me and tell me you'll come. I want to see you and hold you again.

> *Yours forever,*
> *Jacques*

The letter fell from Julia's fingers. Tears streamed down her cheeks. Her sobs echoed off the walls. She needed to get to the phone. She had to tell Jacques that she would be there tomorrow, but she couldn't move. Her body felt like it was permanently rooted to the floor, and there was a vise squeezing her head. Her heart hurt so badly that she was sure it was breaking into a million pieces.

She finally dragged herself out of the chair, staggered to her desk, and dialed the phone. When he answered, all she could manage to say was, "I'm on my way, my love."

The Snow Globe

Christmas was fast approaching. I would soon be back in my childhood home, if everything went as planned.

My travel plans were all in place. I had almost everything packed, and the car was ready, except for loading my suitcases and a few last minute gifts.

I would have almost two weeks with my family!

With only a few things still on my gift list, I decided to head for the mall, where I wandered around looking for something that might catch my fancy. I needed something for my parents and my younger sister.

It was always difficult to shop for them. I mean, what do you get for your parents when they've been married for forty-five years and have everything they could possibly want or need in this lifetime or the next.

I had wandered in and out of half the stores in the mall when I saw a small nondescript store at the far end of the wing I was in. It had a hand-printed sign over the door that said *Kaleidoscopes.* Now that wasn't a kind of shop you came across every day, especially in a mall filled with chain stores.

I walked over to the storefront and saw another sign in the window written in the same script as the sign over the door: *The Answer to All Your Last-Minute Gift Needs.*

I hesitated for a moment, wondering if I should enter. There was something rather eerie about the place.

As I stood there looking in the window of the store, a woman in a faded dress and a tattered shawl stepped to the entryway. She looked at me for what felt like five minutes but was in reality, probably only five seconds

Just as I broke eye contact, she nodded, stepped aside, and waved me in. I paused briefly, then told myself I was being silly. I overcame my uneasiness and stepped inside.

There were so many things crammed into the small space that there wasn't a bare spot on either the walls or the tables.

Sitting on shelves were dolls, hundreds of dolls, all of them very spooky.

Hanging from hooks were equally as many kaleidoscopes. But by far the most abundant item was snow globes. Every inch of floor space was covered with tables, and every table was crammed with them. They ranged in size from as big as a dinner plate to not much bigger than a quarter. I was sure I couldn't even lift the big ones.

I paid no attention to the other items. The only things I was interested in were the snow globes.

I have always been interested in them, as long as they were well made or depicted realistic scenes. These satisfied both my requirements.

As I wandered among the tables, I saw a sign in faded blue ink that read *Snow globes—your town, guaranteed.*

I scoffed at the idea. There was no way they'd have my hometown. I come from a small town in the middle of Wisconsin. But I looked through them anyhow. Imagine my shock when I picked up a medium-sized globe and saw a scene that had been part of my childhood.

As I peered into the globe, I realized that not only was this a scene from my hometown, but also the very street I lived on. There was the house my grandparents had built when they got married. How could this be possible? Maybe it just looked similar. I picked up the globe and up-ended it. There was a sticker on the bottom: *December in New Holstein, Wisconsin.*

I flipped it upright and noticed that the scene had changed. It was still New Holstein, but this time it was Main Street at Christmastime. I recognized the bright, but rather shabby-looking decorations hanging haphazardly on the lightposts.

How could this be? How could the scene have changed? Snow globes don't just change as you flip them.

I almost dropped it. I decided that I would just put it down carefully and leave this place, but for some reason I held onto it. I walked slowly up to the check-out counter. The woman who had invited into the store stood behind the counter.

The smile on her face was pleasant, but not overly so.

"Did you find what you were looking for? If not, I can get it for you."

"Yes, I found what I wanted. Thank You."

Was that a smirk on her face as she wrapped the globe in paper and put it in a bag. She pushed the bag across the counter, I almost shoved it back and left, but something made me hesitate. I took out my credit card and handed it to her.

While she was ringing up the sale, I asked, "Why is this place called Kalidescopes, when you display many more snow globes than kalidescopes?"

She paused, looked at me with that same eerie expression, muttered, "Well dearie, that's a puzzle," and continued the transaction. I took the receipt from her, signed it and handed it back. As I turned toward the door, she grabbed my arm and asked if I would like a box to put it in; it would be easier to wrap.

I pulled my arm from her grip, said no, and made a dash for the door. I heard her chuckle as I stepped outside.

I hurried through the mall. When I reached the corner that led to the outer doors, I glanced back and nearly screamed.

The shop was not there. I was looking at a blank wall! How could that be? I just stepped out of the store, and now there was nothing there but a blank wall?

As I stood there shaking, I thought I heard a chuckle reverberating around me. I shivered and hurried outside. I immediately felt better. The sunlight, the breeze, and the birdsong brought me back to normality.

I drove back to my apartment, carefully put the snow globe in the bottom of my suitcase, then put the suitcase in my the car.

I curled up in my chair with a cup of hot tea and replayed the afternoon at the mall.

That strange, eerie, scary store! And the old woman working in it! That's one store I don't want to enter ever again, though from what I saw as I left the mall, I don't think that will be a problem. What in the world had happened this afternoon? Did I really enter a store that vanished after I bought something? Impossible. My eyes must have been playing tricks on me.

The next morning, after a restless night, I drove off, feeling uneasy. After three days of steady driving, I reached my destination, my childhood home. I was stunned as I neared town. The first thing I usually saw at this point was the small airport and its clump of hangars with their backs to the road. But there was no airport in sight. Instead, there were numerous houses and, of all things, the lumberyard. The high school, which should have been just past the airport, was nowhere to be seen.

Nothing was where it was supposed to be. And everything was where it shouldn't be. What was going on here? Could this have anything to do with that darned snow globe?

The stores that had been arrayed along the upper part of the road were now scattered all over town. Some appeared amongst the businesses (or where the businesses were supposed to be), but others were in the industrial park. Still others were strewn around a former residential area.

The odd thing was that everything was intact. There was no visible damage to any of the buildings.

This hadn't been the result of some destructive natural event like a tornado or an earthquake.

I drove around until I found my family home—at the opposite end of town from where it had been. I pulled up and parked across the street in front of the hardware store that used to be in the middle of Main Street.

My parents must have been watching for me, because when I reached the top step of the porch, Mom pulled the door open and gave me a huge hug. It was a hug that made up for two year's absence. She swung me around and into Dad's arms for a bear hug. Oh, it was good to be home, but why weren't they more worried about the condition of the town?

Before I had a chance to mention the strange juxtaposition, Mom said she had a pot of soup on the stove. Would I like some?

"Is it your beef soup?"

She lauhed, "What else would I make when everyone comes home?"

"Yes please," I smiled. Nothing says 'we're glad you're home' like a big pot of your delicious beef soup."

We sat down and enjoyed a meal of soup and sandwiches and wonderful conversation. We stayed up late, catching up on the past two years. I found out who had passed away, who had new additions to their families, and where many of my friends were now. There is a lot of information that doesn't get passed along in letters.

I woke early the next morning, hoping that everything I had seen on my arrival had been a dream… or a nightmare.

After dressing for the day, I stepped into the hallway, hoping that when I looked out of the window, everything would be as it should have been.

What really stumped me was that no one else seemed to be aware of the alteration in the town. Everyone went about their business as though the world around them was perfectly normal. I, on the other hand, had no idea what was going on.

How could the whole town be turned upside down and no one even notice it? But, even more troubling: *how* could the whole town be turned upside down?

By this time, I had reached the bottom of the stairs and reluctantly lifted my eyes to the front door. It hadn't been a dream. Everything was as displaced as it had been when I drove into town yesterday.

I decided not to mention the situation. I would only talk about it if someone else brought up the subject.

The rest of the family arrived over the next few days and no one mentioned the change.

We spent the days leading up to Christmas in the usual way:in loud, serious, and very heated discussions. We are all opinionated and not afraid to let everyone else know what we think. At the same time, we could happily work and play together, whether cooking in the kitchen or putting together the giant jigsaw puzzle in the parlor. Woven in amongst all of the hustle and bustle, was the mainstay of our gatherings— Mom's soup.

There was always a pot of it sitting on the unheated back porch throughout the day. Anyone who was hungry, or who had children that needed to be fed, could scoop out what they needed and be well satisfied. But mostly, it meant that Mom didn't have to spend all of her time in the kitchen.

After several days of settling in, my sister and I drove off to do some last-minute shopping. There's always more last-minute shopping to do, and we were always up for an adventure.

As we drove off, I couldn't help but notice the alteration in our surroundings, but no one else seemed to be aware of them, so I kept my mouth shut, on that subject at least.

When we got back to town, I nearly drove off into the ditch. There had been another alteration in New Holstein's layout. The businesses that had been mostly in the business park, were now randomized amongst the houses and the empty lot where the high school had been. One of the manufacturing plants had been set down intact, on the railroad tracks on the east end of town. The road that ran directly through town and out east to the next town across those tracks, now veered south and wandered off to who knows where.

I carried my purchases to my bedroom and dropped the bags on the bed. As I turned to grab the scissors off the desk, I noticed a piece of paper lying on the floor partway under the bed.

I picked it up, looked at it carefully and saw that it was the receipt from Kalidescopes. *Hmmm, I thought I threw that out. I must have left it in my shoulder bag instead. I guess it fell out when I grabbed the bag this morning.*

As I went to lay it on the desk, I saw some printing on the back. I didn't remember seeing any writing on the back when I signed it. *I guess I should see what it says.*

I turned it over and read the following: *The bearer of this receipt agrees to keep the origin of this purchase secret. The purchaser also agrees not to hold the seller responsible for the effects caused by the use of the product. The signature on the front of this receipt is legal and binding.* What? What in the world was this all about? What did it mean, 'not responsible for the effects caused by the use of this product?' That wasn't there when I signed it. I was sure the back of the receipt had been blank.

I guess there's nothing I can do about it. The store is gone, and I signed the receipt. I guess I'll be more careful next time.

Over the course of my vacation, I saw exactly what could happen when the snow globe was moved or even just bumped. I would have to put it somewhere that it couldn't be moved, but first, I had to check to be sure. I picked up the globe, turned it upside down and sideways and set it back down.

Then I opened the door. My room was no longer at the end of the hallway, it was in the middle of the hallway. My sister's room was where mine had been, and my parents' was where the upstairs landing had been. The stairway was across the hall from my room.

I crept downstairs. The kitchen, normally beyond the den, was now where the living room had been.

I peered cautiously into the kitchen, not knowing what I would see. There was my mother, calmly making sandwiches for the noon meal. I saw a pot of soup on the stove, and I knew it was beef. At least something appeared to be normal! My older sister was helping mom with lunch, and my brother was leaning back in a chair, regaling them with tall tales.

I stepped into the room with a fake smile plastered on my face. "Hi, how are y'all doing? Anything I can do to help?"

My mother: "No, just sit down and keep us company."

My sister: "Yes, get out the plates and bowls."

My brother: "Hi, Squirt. As long as you're up, why don't you get me a Coke?"

Me: "I'll get the plates and bowls and then sit down and keep y'all company. As for you, brother of mine, get your own Coke, ya' lazy bum."

Mom pretended to be shocked by the exchange, my sister chortled and gave me a thumbs up, and my brother stood up, walked to the refrigerator, grabbed two cans of soda, tossed one to me, and said, "Can I get anything for you two lovely ladies?"

My sister: "I'll have a diet."

My mother: "Thank you, no."

I watched that scene play out before me and wanted to scream out, *"Can't you see that everything is different? Don't you care?"* But I controlled the urge and acted as if everything was normal.

My sister and I did the dishes and got ready to drive to the grocery store to pick up a pork roast for Mom. I was afraid to leave the house. I knew that things would be altered at some point in our outing.

I dashed upstairs, grabbed my purse off the desk, and knocked the snow globe onto the floor. That time I felt the change happen. For just a second, everything shimmered, and then the house shook, almost imperceptibly.

I walked slowly to the door, cracked it open and peeked out into the hallway. Whew! Maybe this time it was just a minor glitch.

As I approached the front door, I tensed. This was the moment. I pulled the door open and— "Are you all right?" asked a man's voice. "You opened the door, yelled NO! and fainted. What happened?"

I was looking up into my father's face. He looked concerned, but not as much as he should be, considering that just outside the front door was sand and cacti!

I mumbled something about being overly tired and, as he helped me up, a shiver and a feeling of dread ran up my spine. I slowly climbed the stairs to my room, with the help of my father and brother. After several hours of sleep, I rose and shakily crept downstairs.

The house was quiet, and I looked around for the sight of anyone. I was beginning to think that they had all disappeared, when I heard the murmur of voices in the parlor. I didn't know how to explain what had happened, so I stuck my head through the door and said,"I'm going out for a walk. I think the fresh air will do me good. I won't be gone long. I'm fine; the rest helped. See you later."

Mom just nodded, dad waved casually, and my brother shifted uneasily in his chair and mumbled.

I backed out of the room, picked up my sunglasses and a bottle of water. I left my jacket on the back of the chair, and stepped out the back door into warm sunshine, *in the middle of December!* Crazy!

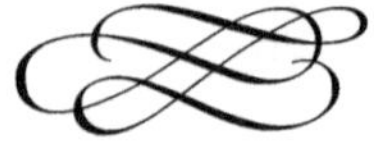

Mom's Beef Soup and Dumplings

**Guaranteed to lessen the trauma of all illnesses,
whether mental or physical**

The Soup

1 chuck roast (2-4 lb.) bone-in if possible
1 celery heart
1 medium onion, cut into 1" cubes
2 whole bay leaves
Salt and pepper to taste
3-4 cups beef broth

◆ Combine the ingredients in a Dutch oven or soup
pot. Bring to a boil, lower the heat, and simmer
for 3-4 hours or until meat is tender. It should fall
apart when lifted out of the pot. Add more water, a
cup or so at a time, as needed.

◆ While the meat is cooking, prepare the following:

> 3-4 medium potatoes, peeled and cut into 1" chunks
>
> 3-4 medium carrots, peeled and cut into 1" chunks, or a small handful of baby carrots, cut in half
>
> 1-2 ribs celery cut into ½" slices
>
> (You may add other vegetables if desired.)

◆ Drop the vegetables into the pot, add 1-2 handfuls of long-grain white rice and 1 handful of barley. Allow to cook until vegies are tender. Meanwhile, cut meat into chunks or pull apart into bite sized pieces, return to Dutch oven. Bring to a boil (add water or broth if needed) Broth will begin to get cloudy looking and thicken slightly from starch in potatoes and rice. Add broth or water as needed. Add salt and pepper if needed.

~

The Dumplings

¾   cup flour
½   teaspoon salt
1   tablespoon vegetable shortening, such as Crisco (Do not use oil, margarine or butter.)
2/3 cup of hot broth from the beef soup
1   lightly beathen egg

◆ Mix together the flour, salt, and shortening until blended.

◆ Add the broth and mix until smooth.

◆ Add the lightly beaten egg and stir until smooth. (Batter will be slightly thinner than pancake batter.)

◆ Drop by spoonfuls into the soup. Use a teaspoon for small dumplings and a tablespoon for larger ones.

◆ Dip spoon into soup each time before scooping batter.

◆ Cover and simmer 10 minutes. Turn dumplings over, cover and cook 10 min. longer.

◆ Cool leftover soup and refrigerate.

May freeze leftovers for up to 6 months

I hope you love this as much as we all do.

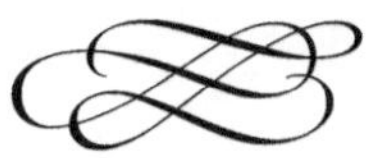